The Nine Classic
Little Golden Books®

The POKY
LITTLE PUPPY
and FRIENDS

A GOLDEN BOOK • NEW YORK

CONTENTS

THE SHY LITTLE KITTEN

Way up in the hayloft of an old red barn lived a mother cat and her new baby kittens. There were five bold and frisky little roly-poly black and white kittens, and *one* little striped kitten who was very, very shy.

One day, the five bold little roly-poly black
and white kittens and the one little roly-poly
striped kitten who was very, very shy all sat
down and washed their faces and paws with

busy little red tongues. They smoothed down
their soft baby fur and stroked their whiskers
and followed their mother down the ladder from
the hayloft—jump, jump, jump!

Then off they marched, straight out of the cool, dark barn, into the warm sunshine. How soft the grass felt under their paws! The five bold and frisky little kittens rolled over in the grass and kicked up their heels with joy.

But the shy little striped kitten just stood off by herself at the very end of the line.

That was how she happened to see the earth
push up in a little mound right in front of her.
Then—*pop!*—up came a pointed little nose.
The nose belonged to a chubby mole.

"Good morning!" said the mole, as friendly as you please. "Won't you come for a walk with me?"

"Oh," said the shy little kitten. She looked shyly over her shoulder.

But the mother cat and her five bold and frisky kittens had disappeared from sight.

So the shy little kitten went walking with
the chubby mole. Soon they met a speckled frog
sitting near the pond.

"My, what big eyes he has!" whispered the shy
little kitten. But the frog had sharp ears, too.

He chuckled. "My mouth is much bigger.
Look!" And the frog opened his great cave of
a mouth.

The mole and the kitten laughed and laughed
until their sides ached.

When the kitten stopped laughing and looked around, the frog had vanished. On the pond, ripples spread out in great silver circles.

"I really should be getting back to my mother and the others," said the shy little kitten, "but I don't know where to find them."

"I'll show you," said a strange voice. And out of the bushes bounded a shaggy black puppy.

"Oh, thank you," said the shy little kitten. "Good-bye, mole."

So off they went together, the shy kitten and the shaggy puppy dog. The little kitten, of course, kept her eyes shyly on the ground.

But the shaggy puppy stopped to bark,
"Woof, woof," at a red squirrel in a tree.
He was full of mischief.

"Chee, chee, chee," the squirrel chattered
back. And she dropped a hickory nut right on
the puppy's nose. She was very brave.

"Wow, wow, wow," barked the mischievous puppy, and off they went toward the farm.

Soon they came bounding out of the woods, and there before them stretched the farmyard.

"Here we are," said the shaggy puppy dog.
So down the hillside they raced, across the
bridge above the brook, and straight on into
the farmyard.

In the middle of the farmyard was the mother cat with her five bold and frisky little black and white kittens. In a flash, the mother cat was beside her shy kitten, licking her all over with a warm red tongue.

"Where have you been?" she cried. "We're all ready to start on a picnic."

The picnic was for all the farmyard animals.
There were seeds for the chickens, water bugs for
the ducks, and carrots and cabbages for the rabbits.
There were flies for the frog, and there was a
trough of mash for the pig.

Yum, yum, yum! How good it all was!

After they had finished eating, everyone was just beginning to feel comfortable and drowsy, when suddenly the frog jumped straight into the air, eyes almost popping out of his head.

"Help! Run!" he cried.

The frog made a leap for the brook.

Everyone scrambled after him and tumbled into the water.

"What is it?" asked the shy little kitten.

"A bee!" groaned the frog. "I bit a bee!"

Then they saw that one side of his mouth was puffed up like a green balloon.

Everybody laughed. They couldn't help it. Even
the frog laughed. They all looked so funny as they
climbed out of the brook.

The shy little kitten stood off to one side.
She felt so good that she turned a backward
somersault, right there in the long meadow
grass. "This is the best day ever," said the
shy little kitten.

The POKY LITTLE PUPPY

Five little puppies dug a hole under the fence and went for a walk in the wide, wide world.

Through the meadow they went, down the road, over the bridge, across the green grass, and up the hill, one right after the other.

And when they got to the top of the hill, they
counted themselves: *one, two, three, four.* One little
puppy wasn't there.

"Now where in the world is that poky little
puppy?" they wondered. For he certainly wasn't on
top of the hill.

He wasn't going down the other side. The only thing they could see going down was a fuzzy caterpillar.

He wasn't coming up this side. The only thing
they could see coming up was a quick green lizard.

But when they looked down at the grassy place near the bottom of the hill, there he was, running round and round, his nose to the ground.

"What is he doing?" the four little puppies asked
one another. And down they went to see, roly-poly,
pell-mell, tumble-bumble, till they came to the
green grass; and there they stopped short.

"What in the world are you doing?" they asked.

"I smell something!" said the poky little puppy.

Then the four little puppies began to sniff, and they smelled it, too.

"Rice pudding!" they said.

And home they went, as fast as they could go, over the bridge, up the road, through the meadow, and under the fence. And there, sure enough, was dinner waiting for them, with rice pudding for dessert.

But their mother was greatly displeased. "So you're the little puppies who dig holes under fences!" she said. "No rice pudding tonight!" And she made them go straight to bed.

But the poky little puppy came home after everyone was sound asleep.

He ate up the rice pudding and crawled into bed as happy as a lark.

The next morning someone had filled the hole and put up a sign. The sign said:

BUT.....
The five little puppies dug a hole under the fence, just the same, and went for a walk in the wide, wide world.

Through the meadow they went, down the road, over the bridge, across the green grass, and up the hill, two and two. And when they got to the top of the hill, they counted themselves: *one, two, three, four.* One little puppy wasn't there.

"Now where in the world is that poky little puppy?" they wondered. For he certainly wasn't on top of the hill.

He wasn't going down the other side. The only thing they could see going down was a big black spider.

He wasn't coming up this side. The only thing they could see coming up was a brown hop-toad.

But when they looked down at the grassy place near the bottom of the hill, there was the poky little puppy, sitting still as a stone, with his head on one side and his ears cocked up.

"What is he doing?" the four little puppies asked one another. And down they went to see, roly-poly, pell-mell, tumble-bumble, till they came to the green grass; and there they stopped short.

"What in the world are you doing?" they asked.

"I hear something!" said the poky little puppy.

The four little puppies listened, and they could hear it, too. "Chocolate custard!" they cried. "Someone is spooning it into our bowls!"

And home they went as fast as they could
go, over the bridge, up the road, through the
meadow, and under the fence. And there,
sure enough, was dinner waiting for them,
with chocolate custard for dessert.

But their mother was greatly displeased. "So you're the little puppies who *will* dig holes under fences!" she said. "No chocolate custard tonight!" And she made them go straight to bed.

But the poky little puppy came home after everyone else was sound asleep, and he ate up all the chocolate custard and crawled into bed as happy as a lark.

The next morning someone had filled the hole and put up a sign.

The sign said:

BUT. . .

In spite of that, the five little puppies dug a hole under the fence and went for a walk in the wide, wide world.

Through the meadow they went, down the road, over the bridge, across the green grass, and up the hill, two and two. And when they got to the top of the hill, they counted themselves: *one, two, three, four.* One little puppy wasn't there.

"Now where in the world is that poky little puppy?" they wondered. For he certainly wasn't on top of the hill.

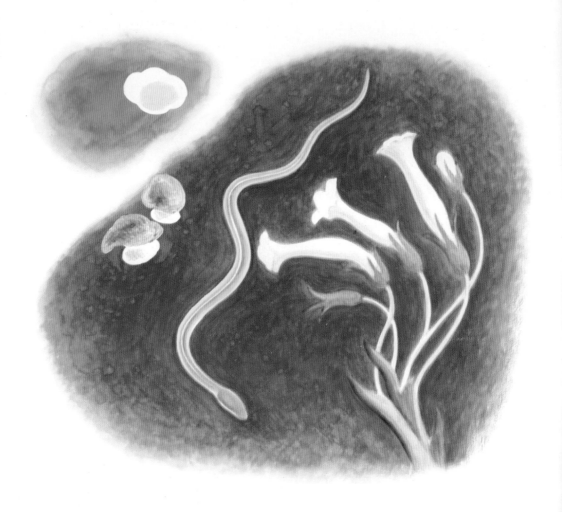

He wasn't going down the other side. The only thing they could see going down was a little grass snake.

He wasn't coming up this side. The only thing they could see coming up was a big grasshopper.

But when they looked down at the
grassy place near the bottom of the hill,
there he was, looking hard at something
on the ground in front of him.

"What is he doing?" the four little
puppies asked one another. And down
they went to see, roly-poly, pell-mell,
tumble-bumble, till they came to the
green grass; and there they stopped short.

"What in the world are you doing?"
they asked.

"I see something!" said the poky little puppy.

The four little puppies looked, and they could see it, too. It was a ripe, red strawberry growing there in the grass.

"Strawberry shortcake!" they cried.

And home they went as fast as they could go, over the bridge, up the road, through the meadow, and under the fence. And there, sure enough, was dinner waiting for them, with strawberry shortcake for dessert.

But their mother said: "So you're the little puppies who dug that hole under the fence again! No strawberry shortcake for supper tonight!" And she made them go straight to bed.

But the four little puppies waited till they thought she was asleep, and then they slipped out and filled up the hole, and when they turned around, there was their mother watching them.

"What good little puppies!" she said. "Come have some strawberry shortcake!"

And this time, when the poky little puppy got home, he had to squeeze in through a wide place in the fence. And there were his four brothers and sisters, licking the last crumbs from their saucer.

"Dear me!" said his mother. "What a pity you're so poky! Now the strawberry shortcake is all gone!"

So the poky little puppy had to go to bed without a single bite of shortcake, and he felt very sorry for himself.

And the next morning someone had put up a sign that read:

NO DESSERTS EVER UNLESS PUPPIES NEVER DIG HOLES UNDER THIS FENCE AGAIN!

THE SAGGY BAGGY
ELEPHANT

A happy little elephant was dancing through the jungle. He thought he was dancing beautifully, one-two-three-kick. But whenever he went one-two-three, his big feet pounded so that they shook the whole jungle. And whenever he went kick, he kicked over a tree or a bush.

The little elephant danced along leaving wreckage behind him, until one day, he met a parrot.

"Why are you shaking the jungle all to pieces?" cried the parrot, who had never before seen an elephant. "What kind of animal are you, anyway?"

The little elephant said, "I don't know what
kind of animal I am. I live all alone in the jungle.
I dance and I kick—and I call myself Sooki.
It's a good-sounding name, and it fits me, don't
you think?"

"Maybe," answered the parrot, "but if it does
it's the only thing that *does* fit you. Your ears are
too big for you, and your nose is way too big for
you. And your skin is *much*, MUCH too big for
you. It's baggy and saggy. You should call yourself
Saggy-Baggy!"

Sooki sighed. His pants *did* look pretty
wrinkled.

"I'd be glad to improve myself," he said, "but I
don't know how to go about it. What shall I do?"

"I can't tell you. I never saw anything like you
in all my life!" replied the parrot.

The little elephant tried to smooth out his skin.
He rubbed it with his trunk. That did no good.

He pulled up his pants legs—but they fell right back into dozens of wrinkles.

It was very disappointing, and the parrot's saucy laugh didn't help a bit.

Just then a tiger came walking along. He was a beautiful, sleek tiger. His skin fit him like a glove.

Sooki rushed up to him and said:

"Tiger, please tell me why your skin fits so well! The parrot says mine is all baggy and saggy, and I do want to make it fit me like yours fits you!"

The tiger didn't care a fig about Sooki's troubles, but he did feel flattered and important, and he did feel just a little mite hungry.

"My skin always did fit," said the tiger. "Maybe it's because I take a lot of exercise. But . . ." added the tiger, ". . . if you don't care for exercise, I shall be delighted to nibble a few of those extra pounds of skin off for you!"

"Oh no, thank you! No, thank you!" cried Sooki. "I love exercise! Just watch me!"

Sooki ran until he was well beyond reach.

Then he did somersaults and rolled on his back. He walked on his hind legs and he walked on his front legs.

When Sooki wandered down to the river to get a big drink of water, he met the parrot. The parrot laughed harder than ever.

"I tried exercising," sighed the little elephant. "Now I don't know what to do."

"Soak in the water the way the crocodile does," laughed the parrot. "Maybe your skin will shrink."

So Sooki tramped straight into the water.

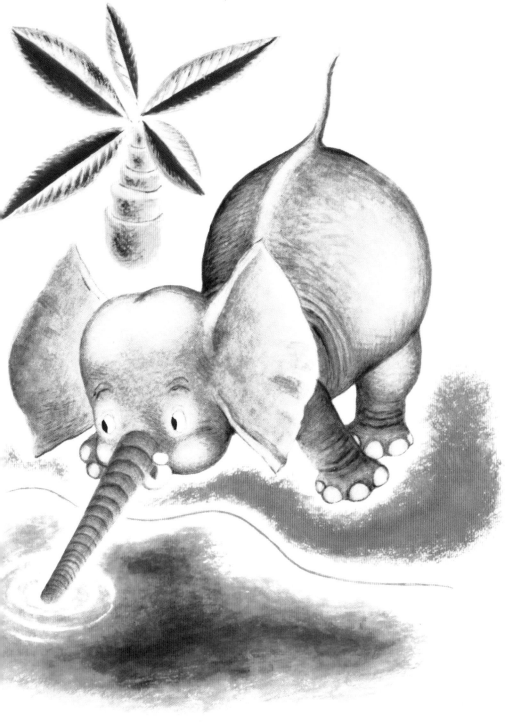

But before he had soaked nearly long enough
to shrink his skin, a great big crocodile came
swimming up, snapping his fierce jaws and looking
greedily at Sooki's tender ears.

The little elephant clambered up the bank and ran away, feeling very discouraged.

"I'd better hide in a dark place where my bags and sags and creases and wrinkles won't show," he said.

By and by he found a deep dark cave, and with a heavy sigh he tramped inside and sat down.

Suddenly, he heard a fierce growling and grumbling and snarling. He peeped out of the cave and saw a lion padding down the path.

"I'm hungry!" roared the lion. "I haven't had a thing to eat today. Not a thing except a thin, bony antelope, and a puny monkey—and a buffalo, but such a tough one! And two turtles, but you can't count turtles. There's nothing much to eat between those saucers they wear for clothes! I'm *hungry!* I could eat an *elephant!*"

And he began to pad straight toward the dark cave where the little elephant was hidden.

"This is the end of me, sags, bags, wrinkles and all," thought Sooki, and he let out one last, trumpeting bellow!

Just as he did, the jungle was filled with a terrible crashing and an awful stomping. A whole herd of great gray wrinkled elephants came charging up, and the big hungry lion jumped up in the air, turned around, and ran away as fast as he could go.

Sooki peeped out of the cave and all the big elephants smiled at him. Sooki thought they were the most beautiful creatures he had ever seen.

"I wish I looked just like you," he said.

"You do," grinned the big elephants. "You're a perfectly dandy little elephant!"

And that made Sooki so happy that he began to

dance one-two-three-kick through the jungle, with
all those big, brave, friendly elephants behind him.
The saucy parrot watched them dance. But this time
he didn't laugh, not even to himself.

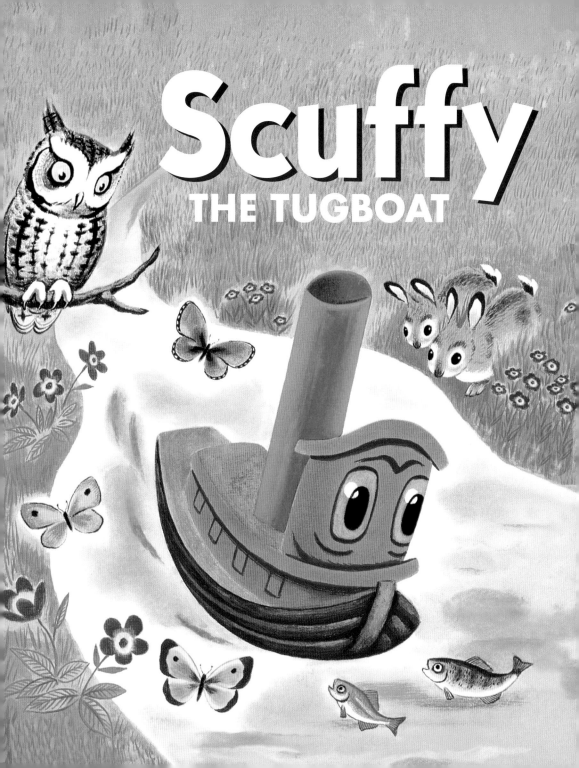

Scuffy
THE TUGBOAT

Scuffy was sad.
Scuffy was cross.
Scuffy sniffed his blue smokestack.

"A toy store is no place for a red-painted tugboat,"
said Scuffy, and he sniffed his blue smokestack again.
"I was meant for bigger things."

"Perhaps you would not be cross if you went sailing," said the man with the polka dot tie, who owned the shop.

So one night he took Scuffy home to his little boy. He filled the bathtub with water.

"Sail, little tugboat," said the little boy.

"I won't sail in a bathtub," said Scuffy. "A tub is no place for a red-painted tugboat. I was meant for bigger things."

The next day the man with the polka dot tie and his little boy carried Scuffy to a laughing brook that started high in the hills.

"Sail, little tugboat," said the man with the polka dot tie.

It was Spring, and the brook was full to the brim with its water. And the water moved in a hurry, as all things move in a hurry when it is Spring.

Scuffy was in a hurry, too.

"Come back, little tugboat, come back," cried the little boy as the hurrying, brimful brook carried Scuffy downstream.

"Not I," tooted Scuffy. "Not I. This is the life for me."

All that day Scuffy sailed along with the brook.

Past the meadows filled with cowslips. Past the
women washing clothes on the bank. Past the
little woods filled with violets.

Cows came to the brook to drink.

They stood in the cool water, and it was fun

to sail around between their legs and bump softly
into their noses.

It was fun to see them drink.

But when a white and brown cow almost
drank Scuffy instead of the brook's cool water,
Scuffy was frightened. That was not fun!

Night came, and with it the moon.
There was nothing to see but the quiet trees.
Suddenly an owl called out, "Hoot! Hooot!"
"Toot, tooot!" cried the frightened tugboat,
and he wished he could see the smiling face of
the man with the polka dot tie.

When morning came, Scuffy was cross instead of frightened.

"I was meant for bigger things, but which way am I to go?" he said. But there was only one way to go, and that was with the running water where the two brooks met to form a small river. And with the river sailed Scuffy, the red-painted tugboat.

He was proud when he sailed past villages.
"People build villages at the edge of my river,"
said Scuffy, and he straightened his blue smokestack.

Once Scuffy's river joined a small one jammed with logs. Here were men in heavy jackets and great boots, walking about on the floating logs, trying to pry them free.

"Toot, toot, let me through," demanded Scuffy. But the men paid no attention to him. They pushed the logs apart so they would drift with the river to the sawmill in the town. Scuffy bumped along with the jostling logs.

"Ouch!" he cried as two logs bumped together.

"This is a fine river," said Scuffy, "but it's very busy and very big for me."

He was proud when he sailed under the bridges.

"My river is so wide and so deep that people must build bridges to cross it."

The river moved through big towns now instead of villages.

And the bridges over it were very wide—wide
enough so that many cars and trucks and streetcars
could cross all at once.

The river got deeper and deeper. Scuffy
did not have to tuck up his bottom.

The river moved faster and faster.

"I feel like a train instead of a tugboat,"
said Scuffy, as he was hurried along.

He was proud when he passed the old
sawmill with its water wheel.

But high in the hills and mountains the winter snow melted. Water filled the brooks and rushed from there into the small rivers. Faster and faster it flowed, to the great river where Scuffy sailed.

"There is too much water in this river," said Scuffy, as he pitched and tossed on the waves. "Soon it will splash over the top and what a flood there will be!"

Soon great armies of men came to save the fields and towns from the rushing water.

They filled bags with sand and put them at the edge of the river.

"They're making higher banks for the river," shouted Scuffy, "to hold the water back." The water rose higher and higher.

The men built the sand bags higher and higher. Higher! went the river. Higher! went the sand bags.

At last the water rose no more. The flood water rushed on to the sea, and Scuffy raced along with the flood. The people and the fields and the towns were safe.

On went the river to the sea. At last Scuffy
sailed into a big city. Here the river widened,
and all about were docks and wharves.

Oh, it was a busy place and a noisy place! The cranes groaned as they swung the cargoes into great ships. The porters shouted as they carried suitcases and boxes on board.

Horses stamped and truck motors roared, streetcars clanged and people shouted. Scuffy said, "Toot, toot," but nobody noticed.

"Oh, oh!" cried Scuffy when he saw the sea. "There is no beginning and there is no end to the sea. I wish I could find the man with the polka dot tie and his little boy!"

Just as the little red-painted tugboat sailed past the last piece of land, a hand reached out and picked him up. And there was the man with the polka dot tie, with his little boy beside him.

Scuffy is home now with the man with the
polka dot tie and his little boy.
   He sails from one end of the bathtub to the other.
   "This is the place for a red-painted tugboat,"
said Scuffy. "And this is the life for me."

Far, far to the west of everywhere is the village of Lower Trainswitch. All the baby locomotives go there to learn to be big locomotives. The young locomotives steam up and down the tracks, trying to call out the long, sad *ToooOoooot* of the big locomotives. But the best they can do is a gay little *Tootle.*

Lower Trainswitch has a fine school for engines. There are lessons in Whistle Blowing, Stopping for a Red Flag Waving, Puffing Loudly When Starting, Coming Around Curves Safely, Screeching When Stopping, and Clicking and Clacking Over the Rails.

Of all the things that are taught in the Lower Trainswitch School for Locomotives, the most important is, of course, Staying on the Rails No Matter What.

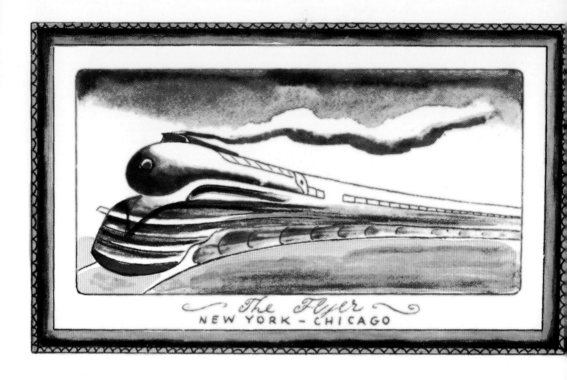

The Flyer
NEW YORK - CHICAGO

The head of the school is an old engineer named
Bill. Bill always tells the new locomotives that he will
not be angry if they sometimes spill the soup pulling
the diner, or if they turn the milk to butter now and
then. But they will never, never be good trains unless
they get 100 A+ in Staying on the Rails No Matter
What. All the baby engines work very hard to get
100 A+ in Staying on the Rails. After a few weeks
not one of the engines in the Lower Trainswitch
School for Trains would even think of getting off
the rails, no matter—well, no matter what.

One day a new locomotive named Tootle came to school.

"Here is the finest baby I've seen since old 600," thought Bill. He patted the gleaming young locomotive and said, "How would you like to grow up to be the Flyer between New York and Chicago?"

"If a Flyer goes very fast, I should like to be one," Tootle answered. "I love to go fast. Watch me."

He raced all around the roundhouse.

"Good! Good!" said Bill. "You must study Whistle Blowing, Puffing Loudly When Starting, Stopping for a Red Flag Waving, and Pulling the Diner without Spilling the Soup.

"But most of all you must study Staying on the Rails No Matter What. Remember, you can't be a Flyer unless you get 100 A+ in Staying on the Rails."

Tootle promised that he would remember and that he would work very hard.

He did, too.

He even worked hard at Stopping for a Red Flag Waving. Tootle did not like those lessons at all. There is nothing a locomotive hates more than stopping.

But Bill said that no locomotive ever, ever kept going when he saw a red flag waving.

One day, while Tootle was practicing for his lesson in Staying on the Rails No Matter What, a dreadful thing happened.

He looked across the meadow he was running through and saw a fine, strong black horse.

"Race you to the river," shouted the black horse, and kicked up his heels.

Away went the horse. His black tail streamed out behind him, and his mane tossed in the wind. Oh, how he could run!

"Here I go," said Tootle to himself.

"If I am going to be a Flyer, I can't let a horse beat me," he puffed. "Everyone at school will laugh at me."

His wheels turned so fast that they were silver streaks. The cars lurched and bumped together. And just as Tootle was sure he could win, the tracks made a great curve.

"Oh, Whistle!" cried Tootle. "That horse will beat me now. He'll run straight while I take the Great Curve."

Then the Dreadful Thing happened. After all that Bill had said about Staying on the Rails No Matter What, Tootle jumped off the tracks and raced alongside the black horse!

The race ended in a tie. Both Tootle and the black horse were happy. They stood on the bank of the river and talked.

"It's nice here in the meadow," Tootle said.

When Tootle got back to school, he said nothing about leaving the rails. But he thought about it that night in the roundhouse.

"Tomorrow I will work hard," decided Tootle.
"I will not even think of leaving the rails, no
matter what."

And he did work hard. He practiced tootling
so much that the Mayor Himself ran up the hill,
his green coattails flapping, and said that everyone
in the village had a headache and would he please
stop TOOTLING.

So Tootle was sent to practice Staying on the
Rails No Matter What.

As he came to the Great Curve, Tootle looked across the meadow. It was full of buttercups.

"It's like a big yellow carpet. How I should like to play in them and hold one under my searchlight to see if I like butter!" thought Tootle. "But no, I am going to be a Flyer and I must practice Staying on the Rails No Matter What!"

Tootle clicked and clacked around the Great Curve. His wheels began to say over and over again, "Do you like butter? Do you?"

"I don't know," said Tootle crossly. "But I'm going to find out."

He stopped much faster than any good Flyer ever does, unless he is stopping for a Red Flag Waving. He hopped off the tracks and bumped along the meadow to the yellow buttercups.

"What fun!" said Tootle.

And he danced around and around and held one of the buttercups under his searchlight.

"I do like butter!" cried Tootle. "I do!"

At last the sun began to go down, and it was time to hurry to the roundhouse.

110

That evening while the Chief Oiler was playing checkers with old Bill, he said, "It's queer. It's very queer, but I found grass between Tootle's front wheels today."

"Hmm," said Bill. "There must be grass growing on the tracks."

"Not on our tracks," said the Day Watchman, who spent his days watching the tracks and his nights watching Bill and the Chief Oiler play checkers.

Bill's face was stern. "Tootle knows he must get 100 A+ in Staying on the Rails No Matter What, if he is going to be a Flyer."

Next day Tootle played all day in the meadow.
He watched a green frog and he made a daisy chain.
He found a rain barrel, and he said softly, "Toot!"
"TOOT!" shouted the barrel. "Why, I sound like a
Flyer already!" cried Tootle.

That night the First Assistant Oiler said he had found a daisy in Tootle's bell. The day after that, the Second Assistant Oiler said that he had found hollyhock flowers floating in Tootle's eight bowls of soup.

And then the Mayor Himself said that he had seen Tootle chasing butterflies in the meadow. The Mayor Himself said that Tootle had looked very silly, too.

Early one morning Bill had a long, long talk with the Mayor Himself.

When the Mayor Himself left the Lower Trainswitch School for Locomotives, he laughed all the way to the village.

"Bill's plan will surely put Tootle back on the track," he chuckled.

Bill ran from one store to the next, buying ten yards of this and twenty yards of that and all you have of the other. The Chief Oiler and the First, Second, and Third Assistant Oilers were hammering and sawing instead of oiling and polishing. And Tootle? Well, Tootle was in the meadow watching the butterflies flying and wishing he could dip and soar as they did.

Not a store in Lower Trainswitch was open the next day and not a person was at home. By the time the sun came up, every villager was hiding in the meadow along the tracks. And each of them had a red flag. It had taken all the red goods in Lower Trainswitch, and hard work by the Oilers, but there was a red flag for everyone.

Soon Tootle came tootling happily down the
tracks. When he came to the meadow, he hopped
off the tracks and rolled along the grass. Just as he
was thinking what a beautiful day it was, a red flag
poked up from the grass and waved hard. Tootle
stopped, for every locomotive knows he must Stop
for a Red Flag Waving.

"I'll go another way," said Tootle.

He turned to the left, and up came another waving red flag, this time from the middle of the buttercups.

When he went to the right, there was another red flag waving.

There were red flags waving from the buttercups, in the daisies, under the trees, near the bluebirds' nest, and even one behind the rain barrel. And, of course, Tootle had to stop for each one, for a locomotive must always Stop for a Red Flag Waving.

"Red flags," muttered Tootle. "This meadow is full of red flags. How can I have any fun?

"Whenever I start, I have to stop. Why did I think this meadow was such a fine place? Why don't I ever see a green flag?"

Just as the tears were ready to slide out of his boiler, Tootle happened to look back over his coal car. On the tracks stood Bill, and in his hand was a big green flag. "Oh!" said Tootle.

He puffed up to Bill and stopped.

"This is the place for me," said Tootle. "There is nothing but red flags for locomotives that get off their tracks."

"Hurray!" shouted the people of Lower Trainswitch, and jumped up from their hiding places. "Hurray for Tootle the Flyer!"

Now Tootle is a famous Two-Miles-a-Minute
Flyer. The young locomotives listen to his advice.

"Work hard," he tells them. "Always remember to
Stop for a Red Flag Waving. But most of all, Stay on
the Rails No Matter What."

Once there were two color kittens with green eyes, Brush and Hush. They liked to mix and make colors by splashing one color into another. They had buckets and buckets

and buckets and buckets of color to splash around
with. Out of these colors they would make all the
colors in the world.

The buckets had the colors written on them, but of course the kittens couldn't read. They had to tell by the colors. "It is very easy," said Brush.

"Red is red. Blue is blue," said Hush.

But they had no green. "No green paint!" said
Brush and Hush. And they wanted green paint,
of course, because nearly every place they liked
to go was green.

Green as cats' eyes
Green as grass
By streams of water
Green as glass.

So they tried to make some green paint.

Brush mixed red paint and white paint together—and what did that make? It didn't make green.

But it made pink.

Pink as pigs

Pink as toes

A PIG

ROSE
A

Pink as a rose
Or a baby's nose.

Then Hush mixed yellow and red together,
and it made orange.

Orange as an orange tree

Orange as a bumblebee

Orange as the setting sun
Sinking slowly in the sea.

The kittens were delighted, but it didn't
make green.

Then they mixed red and blue together—and what did that make? It didn't make green. It made a deep dark purple.

Purple as violets

Purple as prunes

Purple as shadows
On late afternoons.

Still no green! And then . . .

133

O wonderful kittens! O Brush! O Hush!

At last, almost by accident, the kittens poured a bucket of blue and a bucket of yellow together, and it came to pass that they made a green as green as grass.

Green as green leaves on a tree

Green as islands in the sea.

The little kittens were so happy with all the
colors they had made that they began to paint
everything around them. They painted . . .

Green leaves
        and red berries
and purple flowers
        and pink cherries
Red tables
        and yellow chairs
Black trees
        with golden pears.

Then the kittens got so excited they knocked
their buckets upside down and all the colors ran
together. Yellow, red, a little blue, and a little
black . . . and that made brown.

Brown as a tugboat

Brown as an old goat

BROWN

Brown as a beaver

And in all that brown, the sun went down.
It was evening and the colors began to
disappear in the warm dark night.

The kittens fell asleep in the warm dark night
with all their colors out of sight and as they slept
they dreamed their dream—

A wonderful dream
Of a red rose tree
That turned all white
When you counted three

One . . . Two . . .

Three

Of a purple land
In a pale pink sea
Where apples fell
From a golden tree

And then a world of Easter eggs
That danced about on little short legs.

And they dreamed that
A green cat danced
With a little pink dog

Till they all disappeared in a soft gray fog.

And suddenly Brush woke up and Hush woke up. It was morning. They crawled out of bed into a big bright world. The sky was wild with sunshine.

The kittens were wild with purring and pouncing—

Pounce

Pounce

Pounce

They got so pouncy they knocked over the buckets and all the colors ran out together.

There were all the colors in the world and the color kittens had made them.

The Little
RED HEN

One summer day the Little Red Hen found a grain of wheat.

"A grain of wheat!" said the Little Red Hen to herself. "I will plant it."

She asked the duck:
"Will you help me plant this grain of wheat?"
"Not I!" said the duck.

She asked the goose:
"Will you help me plant this grain of wheat?"
"Not I!" said the goose.

She asked the cat:
"Will you help me plant this grain of wheat?"
"Not I!" said the cat.

She asked the pig:
"Will you help me plant this grain of wheat?"
"Not I!" said the pig.

"Then I will plant it myself," said the Little
Red Hen. And she did.

Soon the wheat grew tall, and the Little Red Hen
knew it was time to reap it.

"Who will help me reap the wheat?" she asked.

"Not I!" said the duck.

"Not I!" said the goose.

"Not I!" said the cat.

"Not I!" said the pig.

"Then I will reap it myself,"
said the Little Red Hen.
And she did.

She reaped the wheat, and it was ready to be taken to the mill and made into flour.

"Who will help me carry the wheat to the mill?" she asked.

"Not I!" said the duck.
"Not I!" said the goose.
"Not I!" said the cat.
"Not I!" said the pig.

"Then I will carry it myself," said the Little Red Hen. And she did. She carried the wheat to the mill, and the miller made it into flour.

When she got it home, she asked, "Who will help
me make the flour into dough?"

"Not I!" said the duck.

"Not I!" said the goose.

"Not I!" said the cat.

"Not I!" said the pig.

"Then I will make the dough myself," said the
Little Red Hen. And she did.

Soon the bread was ready to go into the oven.

"Who will help me bake the bread?" said the
Little Red Hen.

"Not I!" said the duck.

"Not I!" said the goose.

"Not I!" said the cat.

"Not I!" said the pig.

"Then I will bake it myself," said the Little Red
Hen. And she did.

After the loaf had been taken from the oven, it
was set on the windowsill to cool.

"And now," said the Little Red Hen, "who will help me eat the bread?"

"I will!" said the duck.

"I will!" said the goose.

"I will!" said the cat.

165

"I will!" said the pig.

"No, I will eat it myself!" said the Little
Red Hen. And she did.

Tenggren's TAWNY SCRAWNY LION

Once there was a tawny, scrawny, hungry lion who never could get enough to eat.

He chased monkeys on Monday—

—kangaroos on Tuesday—

—zebras on Wednesday—

—bears on Thursday—

—camels on Friday—

and on Saturday, elephants!

And since he caught everything he ran after, that lion should have been as fat as butter. But he wasn't at all. The more he ate, the scrawnier and hungrier he grew.

The other animals didn't feel one bit safe. They stood at a distance and tried to talk things over with the tawny, scrawny lion.

"It's all your fault for running away," he grumbled. "If I didn't have to run, run, run for every single bite I get, I'd be fat as butter and

sleek as satin. Then I wouldn't have to eat so much, and you'd last longer!"

Just then, a fat little rabbit came hopping through the forest, picking berries. All the big animals looked at him and grinned slyly.

"Rabbit," they said. "Oh, you lucky rabbit! We appoint you to talk things over with the lion."

That made the little rabbit feel very proud.
"What shall I talk about?" he asked eagerly.

"Any old thing," said the big animals. "The
important thing is to go right up close."

So the fat little rabbit hopped right up to the
big hungry lion and counted his ribs.

"You look much too scrawny to talk things over," he said. "So how about supper at my house first?"

"What's for supper?" asked the lion.

The little rabbit said, "Carrot stew." That sounded awful to the lion. But the little rabbit said, "Yes sir, my five fat sisters and my four fat

brothers are making a delicious big carrot stew right now!"

"What are we waiting for?" cried the lion. And he went hopping away with the little rabbit, thinking of ten fat rabbits, and looking just as jolly as you please.

"Well," grinned all the big animals. "That should take care of Tawny-Scrawny for today."

Before very long, the lion began to wonder if they would ever get to the rabbit's house.

First, the fat little rabbit kept stopping to pick berries and mushrooms and all sorts of good-smelling herbs. And when his basket was full, what did he do but flop down on the river bank!

"Wait a bit," he said.

"I want to catch a few fish for the stew."

That was almost too much for the hungry lion.

For a moment, he thought he would have to eat that one little rabbit then and there. But he kept saying "five fat sisters and four fat brothers" over and over to himself. And at last the two were on their way again.

"Here we are!" said the rabbit, hopping around a turn with the lion close behind him. Sure enough, there was the rabbit's house, with a big pot of carrot stew bubbling over an open fire.

And sure enough, there were nine more fat, merry little rabbits hopping around it!

When they saw the fish, they popped them into the stew, along with the mushrooms and herbs. The stew began to smell very good indeed.

And when they saw the tawny, scrawny lion, they gave him a big bowl of hot stew. And then they hopped about so busily, that really, it would have been quite a job for that tired, hungry lion to catch even one of them!

So he gobbled his stew, but the rabbits filled his bowl again. When he had eaten all he could hold, they heaped his bowl with berries.

And when the berries were gone—the tawny,
scrawny lion wasn't scrawny any more! He felt so good
and fat and comfortable that he couldn't even move.

"Here's a fine thing!" he said to himself. "All these fat little rabbits, and I haven't room inside for even one!"

He looked at all those fine, fat little rabbits and wished he'd get hungry again.

"Mind if I stay a while?" he asked.

"We wouldn't even hear of your going!" said the rabbits. Then they plumped themselves down in the lion's lap and began to sing songs.

And somehow, even when it was time to say
goodnight, that lion wasn't one bit hungry!

Home he went, through the soft moonlight,
singing softly to himself. He curled up in his bed,
patted his sleek, fat tummy, and smiled.

When he woke up in the morning, it was Monday.
"Time to chase monkeys!" said the lion.

But he wasn't one bit hungry for monkeys! What he wanted was some more of that tasty carrot stew. So off he went to visit the rabbits.

On Tuesday he didn't want kangaroos, and on Wednesday he didn't want zebras. He wasn't hungry for bears on Thursday, or camels on Friday, or elephants on Saturday.

All the big animals were so surprised and happy!

They dressed in their best and went to see the fat little rabbit.

"Rabbit," they said. "Oh, you wonderful rabbit! What in the world did you talk to the tawny, scrawny, hungry, terrible lion about?"

The fat little rabbit jumped up in the air and said, "Oh, my goodness! We had such a good time with that nice, jolly lion that I guess we forgot to talk about anything at all!"

And before the big animals could say one word, the tawny lion came skipping up the path. He had a basket of berries for the fat rabbit sisters, and a string of fish for the fat rabbit brothers, and a big bunch of daisies for the fat rabbit himself.

"I came for supper," he said, shaking paws all around.

Then he sat down in the soft grass, looking fat as butter, sleek as satin, and jolly as all get out, all ready for another good big supper of carrot stew.

THE LITTLE RED
Caboose

The little red caboose
always came last.

First came the big black engine,
puffing and chuffing.

Then came the boxcars,

then the oil cars,

then the coal cars,

then the flat cars.
Sometimes they were
switched around in different ways.

But the little red caboose
always came last.

Boys and girls waved at
the big black engine.

They listened to the boxcars
and the oil cars
and the coal cars
and the flat cars
go *clickety clack.*

But by the time the little red caboose
came along, the boys and girls were
turning away.

Because the little red caboose
always came last.

"Oh, smoke!" said the little red caboose.

"I wish I were a flat car or a coal
car or an oil car or a boxcar, so boys
and girls would wave at me.

"How I wish I were a big black
engine, puffing and chuffing way up at
the front of the train!

"But I'm just the little old red caboose.
Nobody cares for me."

One day the train started up a mountain.
Up went the big black engine.
Up went the boxcars.
Up went the oil cars.

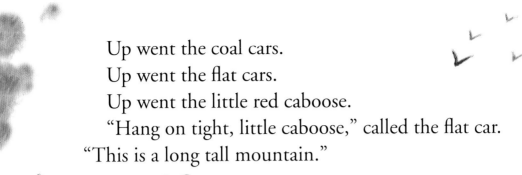

Up went the coal cars.
Up went the flat cars.
Up went the little red caboose.
"Hang on tight, little caboose," called the flat car.
"This is a long tall mountain."

The train went slower and slower and s-l-o-w-e-r.

Soon it was hardly moving.

It looked as if that train could not get up the mountain.

"Look out, little caboose!" called the flat car. "The train is starting to slip back down this long tall mountain!"

"Not if I can help it!" said the little red caboose. And he slammed on his brakes.
And he held tight to the tracks.
And he kept that train from sliding down the mountain!

Then, *bump!*
The little red caboose felt
something push him from behind.

210

It was two big black engines.
They pushed the train up to the top
of the mountain.

"We couldn't have done it,"
said the big black engines,
"if it had not been for the
little red caboose."
Everyone cheered.
And the little red caboose
nearly burst with pride.

Now, children wave at the big
black engine and at all the cars.

But they save their biggest waves for the little red caboose. Because the little red caboose saved the train.